characters created by Lauren Child

I Completely

LOVE winter

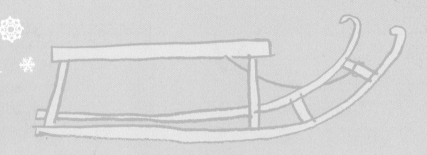

PUFFIN BOOKS
Published by the Penguin Group: London, New York, Australia,
Canada, India, Ireland, New Zealand and South Africa
Penguin Books Ltd, Registered Offices: 80 Strand, London WC2R 0RL, England

puffinbooks.com

I Really, Really Need Actual Ice Skates first published in 2009
Snow is my Favourite and my Best first published in 2006
This collection first published 2013
003
Text and illustrations copyright © Lauren Child/Tiger Aspect Productions Limited, 2006, 2009
Charlie and Lola word and logo ® and © Lauren Child, 2005
Charlie and Lola is produced by Tiger Aspect Productions
All rights reserved
The moral right of the author/illustrator has been asserted
Made and printed in China
ISBN: 978-0-718-19917-3

Text based on script written by Samantha Hill

Illustrations from the TV animation produced by Tiger Aspect Productions Limited

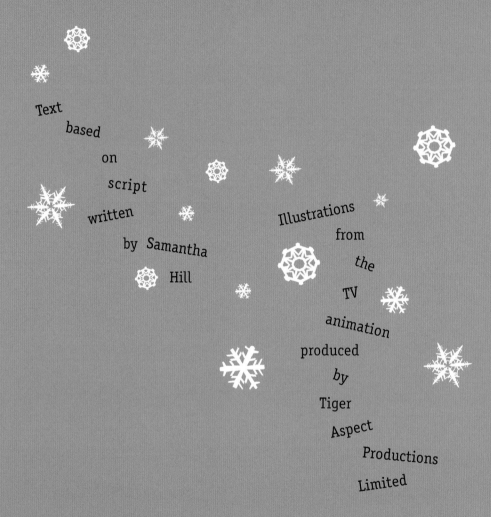

I have this little sister Lola.
    She is small and very funny.
Today Lola is extremely excited
    because the man on the weather
says it's going to snow.

Lola cannot wait for the snow to come.

She says, "Snow is my favourite

and is my best."

I say, "Remember, Lola,

snow can only come when it is very, very cold.

Dad said it might not snow until midnight.

Or even tomorrow."

"I know," says Lola, "but it is **extremely cold** right **now**. So I think the **snow** will come sooner rather than **midnight**."

At bedtime, Lola says,
    "Do you think it has
started snowing now, Charlie?"

"No, go to sleep, Lola."

She says, "I can't because
        it might come while
I'm asleep, sleeping.

I'll just do one more
check...
        No snow.
        Not yet."

"See?" I say.
"Go to sleep."

But a little bit later
I hear Lola creeping
out of bed again.

"Ooooh!" she says.
"It's SnOWing!
Charlie, come quick.
It's SnOWing, it's really,
really SnOWing!"

So I watch the snow with Lola.
She says, "Can we go out
and play in it now?"

"Not now, Lola," I say. "Wait until morning.
Then there'll be more and we can
go on the sledge with Marv and Sizzles.
And you can build a snowman if you want."

In the morning,
Lola shouts,

"Charlie!
Get up, Charlie!
Mum! Dad!

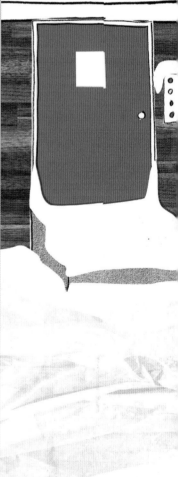

It's all gone
extremely white!"

So Mum and Dad took us to
the park and Lola was right,
everything had turned **extremely**,
completely white.

Then we see Marv and Lotta.
And I say, "Where's Sizzles?"

"Yes," says Lola, "where's Sizzles?"

Marv points to a small pile of snow.
"He's here!"
he says. "Look!"

Lotta and Lola
make snow angels.

Lola says,
"Snow
is my
favourite
and my
best."

"I love **snow!**" says Lotta. "It's my **best** too."

Then we find a big hill and we all
go on the sledge. Even Sizzles!

I say, "Ready?
Steady?
Go!"

Wheeeeeeeee

eeeeee!

Then me and Marv
build a **snowman**.

Lotta says,
"Let's make a
snow doggy.
Come on, Lola!"

Later we go home to have some hot chocolate.

Marv says, "Mmmm. I love hot chocolate!"

Lola says,
"I love snow. Tomorrow I might put snowdog
and Sizzles on the sledge for a ride."

"I'm going to make a snow kennel," says Lotta,
"... and what about snow puppies?"

"Yes!" says Lola. "We can have lots of snow puppies!"

But when we go to the park the next day,
Lola can't make anything.

"It's gone!" she says.

"All the lovely snow is absolutely gone.
There's no more white, Charlie.
It's all cold
                     and wet
            and brown.
        And snowdog's gone."

So we go home again.

Lola says,
"Why can't we
           have **sn**o**w**
eve**ry** day?"

And I say,
"Because it wouldn't be special.
Imagine you had a birthday
every day, so you had parties
and cakes and presents
all the time."

And Lola says,
"What's wr0ng with having

birthdays every day?"

And I say,
"It wouldn't be a treat, would it? I'm not
sure you would like snow every day."

"I would, Charlie," says Lola.
"Snow is my favourite
and is my best."

Then I have a really good idea. "Well, imagine a completely white land...

... where it's snowy and cold every day.
It's called the Arctic."

"Look at the polar bear," says Lola.
"What's he doing, Charlie?"
I say, "He's going for a swim."

"I'd like to go swimming," says Lola.
"Where's the beach?"
I say,
"There isn't a beach, Lola.
It's far too cold for us to go swimming."

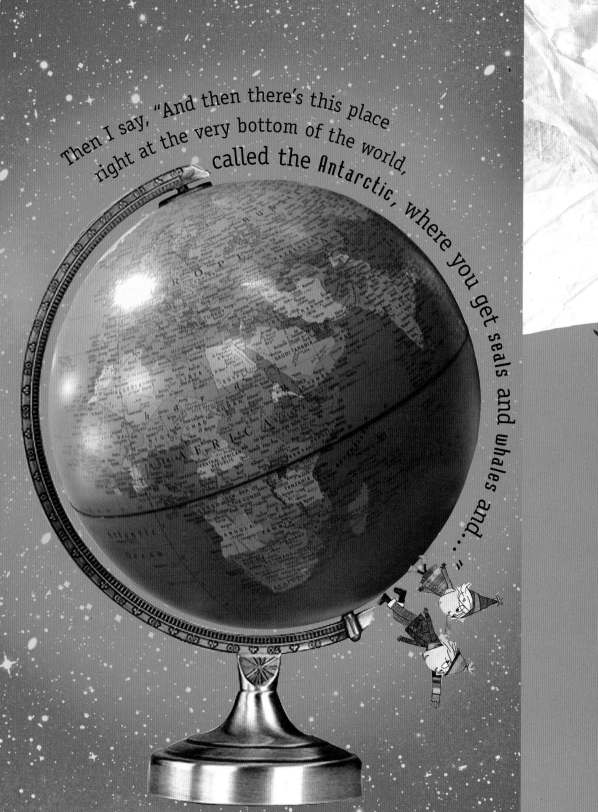

Then I say, "And then there's this place right at the very bottom of the world, called the Antarctic, where you get seals and whales and....."

"Penguins!" says Lola.
"Don't the penguins look smart,
Charlie! They look like they're
going to a party!
I wish I was wearing my best, smartest
party dress, you know, the stripy one."

And I say,
"You couldn't wear your stripy dress in the Antarctic.
You have to wear your coat all the time
because it's so cold."

"Oh yes," says Lola, "I forgot."

Then I say, "But when it's all snowy, you can do this...

...but can we go home now?"

And I say, "But why? I thought snow was your favourite and was your best!"

"Come on!"

And I say, "Isn't it amazing?"

"Wow!" says Lola.

And we slide on the ice with the penguins.

"Yes, Charlie," she

Lola says, "I do like it, Charlie. But I'm just a little chilly!"

"Snow is my favourite and my best, Charlie," says Lola, "but if it was snowy all the time there would be lots of things you couldn't do. So we're maybe lucky, we can do swimming and have stripy dresses and have snow.

But I do feel sad that the snow has all gone."

So I say, "I've got a

rprise for you.
Don't look round!"

"A teeny weeny snowman
who lives in the freezer!"
says Lola. "How did he
get in there?"

"I don't know!" I say.

Lola says, "He's me|t|ing!"
I say, "Shall I put him back
in the freezer so we can keep him?"
"Oh no, Charlie," says Lola.
"Let's watch him me|t!"

I really, REALLY need actual ice skates

Text based on the script written by Bridget Hurst

Illustrations from the TV animation produced by Tiger Aspect Productions Limited

I have this little sister Lola.

She is small and very funny.

Today Lola is really excited.

"Look, Charlie! We've got a letter."

Dear Charlie and Lola,
You remember we promised you some money so you could both buy scooters. Well, here it is. Scoot well.
All our love,
Granny and Grandpa.

"YES!"

says Lola.

And I say,
"I've wanted a
scooter for ages."

When we see Marv and Morten, I can't wait to tell them.

"We're getting **scooters** tomorrow!"

"Great!" says Marv.
"AND my mum is taking
us all to the new
ice-skating rink
after school today."

And Lola says,
"Ooh, ice skating!"

At school, Lola says,
     "Lotta! Lotta! Are you
coming ice skating
          with us today?"

And Lotta says,
"Yes, yes, yes!
     I love ice skating."

Morten says,
"So do I!"

Lola says, "I'm going to do ice skating.

ice twisting...

"Look!" says Lotta.

"Oooh," says Lola. "Evie's got ice skates that are REAL. And I don't have ANY ice skates!"

"But I really do think I need
to have my OWN ice skates,
just like Evie...
with shiny silvery
bits on the bottom,
and ever-so-sparkly laces."

"Don't worry, Lola,"
says Evie.
"You can borrow
ice skates
when you
get to the
ice rink..."

At the ice rink, I say,
    "Come on, Lola!"

And Lola says,
    "It's wobble-ob-erley!"

"Look at me!" says Marv.

"I can do stopping!"
says Morten.

"Ooh, **careful**,"
says Lola.

"Yes, **careful**!"
says Lotta.

"Look at Evie!" says Lola.

"She can go backwardy," says Lotta.

"Yes," says Lola, "backwardy."

Marv says,
"I want to come again REALLY soon!"

"So do I!" says Lotta.

"So do I!" says Morten.

"You know, Charlie, I really do think I absolutely and **EXTREMELY** must have my OWN skates."

"But we're getting the scooters tomorrow... with Dad," I say.

And Lola says, "I'm going to have real ice skates instead of the scooter, Charlie — because then I will be a VERY good and very twirlyish ice-skaterer...

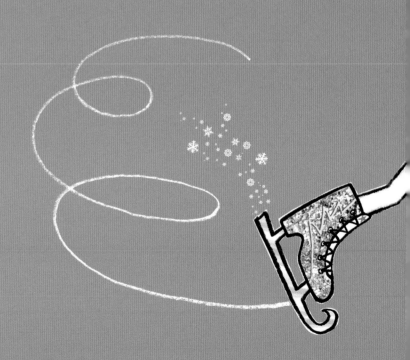

"... I will be the best ice-skaterer

in the WHOLE of the school!"

When we get home, I say,
    "Maybe you should have
ice-skating lessons first,
        in case you don't really
    want them after all..."

And Lola says,
    "But I DO really want them, Charlie!
I really, really, REALLY do!"

"But Lola, what about that **big,** red **kite** you really, really **wanted?**

And that toy **guitar** that you really, REALLY wanted, and never ever really, really played?

AND...

that special lighting-up **yo-yo** you really, really wanted?

You'd better go and ask Dad."

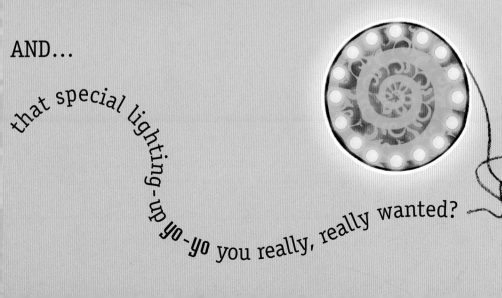

"Dad said yes! Charlie! He said yes!"

"Are you sure, Lola?"

And Lola says,
"Absolutely, completely and EXTREMELY sure.
Dad said I must be very,
very good and promise not to change my
mind and that he doesn't want to find the
skates in the bottom of the cupboard."

Lola says,
        "Do you want to see my
really, really new ice skates?"

And Morten says,
        "They're good, Lola."

        And Lola says,
"I can't wait to do ice skating!"

At the ice rink,
    Lola says,
"Oh!"

And Lotta says,
    "Are your ice skates
good, Lola?"

Lola says,
    "Yes! It's just a little
bit tricky at the moment,
because, you see,
    they have never been
on the ice before..."

And I say,
        "Come on,
hold my **hand**."

Then Lola falls over.
        "I don't want
to have **ice skates**
        any more, Charlie!"

I say,
"You did really, REALLY want ice skates...
        You just have to practise."

And Lola says,
        "Maybe..."

The next time we go ice skating,
Lola sees Morten fall off his scooter.

"Oh!" says Morten.
"I think I don't like scootering very much."

And Lola says, "I don't think I am very
keen on ice skating, actually..."

Do you think our dads would let us do swaps?"

And Morten says,
          "They might!"

"I'm a good scooterer!"
says Lola.

"I'm a really good ice-skate**r**er!"
says Morten.

Then Lola sees Evie...

Boing!

Boing!

and says,
"Oooh!
That looks fun..."